AF437071

I Am a Portrait

ISBN 979-8-218-48179-7

I Am a Portrait

Mary Tonetti Dorra

Contents

The Paris Art Heist

The beautiful Parisian apartment on the posh Avenue Foch, which for 50 years had been the home of Lucie Bernard and her late husband George, was once again readied for Lucie's annual departure to join her cruise ship at Le Havre. It didn't much matter that she was going on the same cruise she had done for the past three years because due to her ever-increasing dementia the trip was always a new experience. Like many who lived on the most affluent street in Paris near the Bois de Boulogne, George had made a great fortune in manufacturing which he left to his adored wife Lucie.

We all gathered in the well-appointed Art Deco living room to enjoy the usual glass of vermouth before going into the dining room for another superb feast. It was always a treat for me to see the three Bonnards dramatically placed together on one wall over the sofa. Two graceful women in lovely print garden dresses looked straight out of their gilt frames at us as if they were part of our party and were waiting to be invited to join us. The third nestled a charming baby to her bosom and was smiling at no one in particular—a touching scene. Lucie's two adult daughters, Yvette and Jacqueline, and their husbands together with the two of us were always invited for the festive last luncheon, before the chauffeur arrived to take Lucie to the airport.

That annual ritual always included a luncheon of some of Lucie's favorite dishes beginning with the first-of-the-season small halves of perfectly ripe Cavaillon melon cupping some of the ruby red port that she always brought back from the cruise stop in Portugal. Suzanne, Lucie's excellent cook then seemed to waltz into the dining room where she proudly served a platter of roasted poulet a *l'estragon en gelee* surrounded by little glistening cubes of jellied chicken broth, and roasted fingerling potatoes next to nests of bright green haricot verts. After the salad and cheese course Lucie smiled as Suzanne once again appeared, with her red curls bobbing on the top of her head. She tripped gaily into the dining room as if appearing on stage with her sensational dessert, a strawberry Charlotte Malakoff which was always as beautiful as it was delicious.

It was sad to say that the Avenue Foch, so quiet during the August month of departures from the "City of Light", had recently become a target for thieves focusing on the empty apartments where everything of value was plundered. The Paris police were at a loss in anticipating which apartments would be the next to be robbed. This news was of course kept from Lucie by her knowledgeable and loving daughters and from Suzanne who would always stay in the maid's room on the floor above while her mistress was away so she could keep watch on the Bernards' apartment.

Suzanne dutifully checked the apartment every day. Only two days after Lucie had departed Suzanne entered the apartment as usual, and gasped when she saw that the three Bonnards had been removed from the wall leaving only the faded marks indicating where they had been. Nothing else had been stolen, she reported in tears to Lucie's older daughter Yvette whom she called immediately. Yvette tried to console the distraught Suzanne on the phone by saying that she would be over that morning and she herself would report it to the police.

* * *

When the police arrived, Suzanne was still in a very frightened state despite Yvette's calm manner and her attempt to soothe the weeping servant. Yvette produced some photos of the missing paintings for the police who said that even though the photos might be helpful, they were still not hopeful of getting the stolen works back. The chief investigator continued, "This kind of robbery has been going on for the past week and I'm afraid there are no clues. Some of the other houses on the Avenue have been robbed of similar works of art."

Suzanne looked frozen as one of the policemen turned to look directly at her and volunteered, "It looks like an inside job." Yvette held onto Suzanne's arm while addressing the policeman sternly, "I don't believe that could be possible here. I'll fill out the report if you leave it with me and I will return it this afternoon to the police station." She led the men abruptly and ceremoniously to the front door. As they left, one of the officers again turned to face Suzanne and with a sly wink, he tipped his hat and smiled, "Au revoir, Madame, a bientôt."

Although at the time I didn't think it was more than a flirtatious gesture, it occurred to me later that the officer was trying to suggest that Suzanne was somehow complicit in the robbery. None of us could accept that possibility because she had been a loyal and trustworthy servant for 40 years. Suzanne's character had been unblemished. What did surprise me was the lack of concern on the part of the Bernard daughters. Those paintings had been valued at over two million francs. When I asked Yvette if they had adequate insurance, she hesitated at first and smiled, "Yes the Bonnards are definitely insured." She continued, "but what is even more important is that Jacqueline and I, motivated by caution, had arranged several years ago, to have the originals placed in the bank and had excellent copies made which we ourselves hung. No one could tell the difference. Not even Lucie."

2

The Call From Haifa

Twenty-six-year-old Rebecca Salama was getting her master's in art history at Northwestern University in Chicago. She was also a docent at the Chicago Art Institute, and her first food blog had become a great success and was beginning to pay off. It was a rainy day in Chicago, and windy too. When the telephone rang she was working at her desk on a paper due the next day.

"Hello. Is this Rebecca Salama, daughter of Raphael and Adrienne Salama?"

Rebecca hesitated only briefly, then in a commanding voice, "Yes. Who is calling?"

'This is Ari Yosef, the lawyer who has been representing the Salama family as part owners of the Haifa property which I discussed with your mother several years ago. Now that your mother is deceased you are one of the two owners of the property, and I have some important news."

Rebecca drew a sharp breath and stood placing both feet firmly on the floor before asking, "What is that news?" her index finger wrapped nervously around a golden curl as she spoke.

"You may remember that there is another owner's name listed with yours, that of Marcel Douek, but neither he nor any of his relatives have ever shown any interest until now. He recently wrote that he would be coming to Tel Aviv to our office next week to discuss the matter of selling the property. We think you should be here too. Is that possible? He wants to sell the entire property that you two own together."

Still standing, Rebecca answered without hesitation, "Of course. I'll be there." She slumped into a chair and stared at nothing, thinking, "I've got to make sure this property doesn't fall into the hands of some self-serving entrepreneur. It is small by American

5

standards, but it has a lovely perspective. The view encompasses the Mediterranean in the distance and overlooks the city of Haifa. I really want to preserve its natural beauty and certainly it should not become the site of another large hotel."

* * *

One week later the lawyer, Ari Yosef, made the introductions in his office. Marcel Douek smiled at Rebecca and rose to shake her hand. She shook his hand cordially but did not smile. Marcel began by saying, "I have been contacted by a third party who has offered a large sum of money in cash to buy our property because he says he really wants it and believes it would be ideal for a Music Academy. Of course, since I am a cellist, I very much would like to see this happen."

"I think it is a very nice idea, but we need to have some guarantee that he will not turn it into a large hotel? How do you know you can trust him? Look at what developers have done to the beautiful island of Mykonos."

Yosef cleared his throat and said, "Rebecca is right. You must be careful. I think she is right to be cautious…even suspicious, and I have ways of finding out about whether we can trust that person or not. In fact, when Marcel mentioned this person in an email to me before you arrived, I looked him up and found him to be a big developer who has already bought many prime properties in Haifa which are being developed into luxury hotels."

Marcel's jaw dropped, "I hadn't thought of that. He did increase the amount he was willing to pay by giving us a bonus of one hundred thousand dollars if the sale to him went through quickly, and I thought that was curious."

Rebecca felt suddenly sorry for him and turned with a softer look towards him, "Marcel, you are a musician and not a businessman. How could you have known? It is still a good idea but we need to find the right people to make the Music Academy become a reality."

Yosef interrupted. "I think I can help with that also, if you would like."

"We have trusted you so far, and I think we do need your help. Marcel, do you agree we should trust Ari by going forward with the plan? We need a buyer who believes in music not more self-serving entrepreneurs."

"I agree. And you are right, Rebecca, I am no businessman!" Marcel added almost inaudibly and without conviction.

Rising from the table, Yosef was smiling at them both and said, "Now it is time for lunch. And it's on me. We've made some progress and should celebrate."

After lunch Marcel turned to face Rebecca, "How long are you staying in Israel? Would you have time to have dinner with me? "Just to get to know each other?" he said smiling at her.

Rebecca nodded, "I'd love that. This evening?"

* * *

When they met at the cozy restaurant overlooking the Haifa coastline, Marcel noticed that Rebecca seemed uneasy. She had taken only a sip of the champagne which Marcel had already ordered. In a staccato voice, she blurted out, "Marcel, I'm really worried about your 'buyer.' I am afraid he is just lying to us and has no intention of making sure a Music Academy would be there. He just wants to build another large hotel on the property the way he has done with other properties in Haifa." Marcel noticed tears were forming in her eyes as she finished this last sentence. Unconsciously he reached across the table in sympathy to hold her hand which she then quickly withdrew.

Rebecca continued, "You know we must have an amendment to the bill of sale stating that the property will be turned into a Music Academy. I felt so strongly about this that I called Yosef and asked him to find the buyer and ask him to sign an amendment ensuring that there would be a Music Academy built on the property. But to add further to his duplicity and strange behavior, the buyer could not be found. He had put the money in escrow in a local bank but then left town. Needless to say, I found that to be very unsettling. Yosef was very sympathetic and said he hadn't trusted the buyer any more than I did and told me not to worry. He had reached out to another potential buyer by the name of George Stavros, whom he believed was entirely trustworthy and who was also interested in talking to us about buying the property and creating a Music Academy on it. There was a tone in his voice that I couldn't trust. I don't know why. But things happen fast when it comes to money around here, and it is so easy to be tricked and maneuvered. Who can we trust? I still think we can trust Ari, but maybe I'm just being naive. Perhaps if we have the guarantee of an amendment attached to the bill of sale, then we will be safe, but who knows?"

Marcel shrugged his shoulders and turned to the waiter who had arrived at the table with menus. "Now let's pause on this subject and have our dinner. Okay? I'm famished."

Early the next morning Rebecca's cell phone was vibrating. She picked it up to see that Ari Yosef was calling. He reported that he hadn't been able to find that original buyer anywhere but that fortunately he had been talking to George Stavros who was extremely interested in the property, but that he didn't want to sign the amendment to guarantee a Music Academy would be built there.

When Rebecca heard this the seed of doubt had grown into a full-size plant. Trusting Ari was no longer possible.

A few days later she called Marcel who listened to her conclusion and not only agreed with her but added dramatically, "Don't you think something is fishy? And get this, Rebecca. I've got news for you. Yosef called last night to let me know that he was resigning as our lawyer without any explanation." Rebecca gasped and they both looked at each other in disbelief.

After a short pause Marcel broke the silence, "The timing suggests something sinister and perhaps it is no coincidence that

Yosef suddenly resigned at the same time of the buyer's refusal to sign the amendment."

"Wait. My phone is vibrating. It is a call from George Stavros. I must take it."

"Hello, Mr. Stavros. Yes this is Rebecca Salama."

"Rebecca, this is George Stavros, the person who is buying your property with Ari Yosef. I just wanted to tell you how pleased I am that you agreed to sell me your property. We are ready to complete the deal."

"What are you talking about? I never signed any papers agreeing to sell the property, Rebecca interjected. George continued, "I became very suspicious of Yosef and thought I should ask you directly if you had changed your mind. But your signature was on the bill of sale, along with Yosef's and Marcel's. Knowing how strongly you felt about there being a Music Academy on the property I thought I should call you directly. Yosef and I are planning to build a beautiful high-rise hotel like the ones we have already built elsewhere in Israel, not a Music Academy."

Rebecca took a deep breath before continuing haltingly. "I would never agree to this. You must cancel the deal because the property is NOT for sale. I will fight this in court if necessary. Marcel's and my signatures must have been forged by Ari."

"That will not be necessary, Rebecca. Rest assured that I want no part of this spurious deal. I am so sorry you had to find out from me that Yosef was so untrustworthy. I had my suspicions about him from the start. But the sale will not go through, and I will have my lawyers cancel everything this afternoon. There are other properties we can consider."

"Thank you, Mr. Stavros. I appreciate your call and your honesty. Thank God, you called me."

When Rebecca communicated the news to Marcel he congratulated her saying, "Neither of us is really desperate for money right now, and the property will only increase in value. So, let's hang on to it…until we find a buyer we can trust to do what we want."

3
Follow Your Passions Even Into Retirement

"Did you come all the way from Brazil to chase butterflies in Santa Barbara?" The aging but still very attractive retired ballerina turned to face the rather short mustachioed man who stood behind her carrying a butterfly net.

"No Madame. I came for the peace and quiet that I assume I will find here at the Casa de Harmonia Retirement home. I am writing a paper on the diversity of the spraghis in blue butterflies or as lepidopterists would call them the Blue Morphos. "He smiled as he curled his mustache and bowed slightly. Allow me to introduce myself, Madame. I am Oskar Lippincott, a dedicated lepidopterist and not from Brazil but rather like the *Morpho helenor guerrensis* I am from Peru. And you are?"

Her lips curled into a small smile as she tried not to giggle. She looked directly at him and drew herself up to her full height. "I am Maria Castellanos de Varga and a ballerina, or at least I used to be. I am no longer a dancer," she added wistfully. "I too am looking for peace and quiet. I have known too many people in my long life and those are mostly dead now. I don't need any other people in my life at the present time…I am too tired for more. But I am intrigued by you and your name. How is it that your name is Lippincott? That doesn't sound Peruvian or Spanish? Please explain how come you have that Anglo Saxon name and yet you are from Peru?"

"My grandfather came from Devon, England in the 1880s as an entrepreneur. He like many in Great Britain was fascinated by the Rubber Boom in Chile and Peru. Before Peru was a country it was known as the Viceroyalty of Peru or the Kingdom of Peru, founded in 1542 and ended with the last vice royal Pio de Tristan in 1824, when Peru became independent from Spain. My grandfather, a young Anglo Saxon, was an adventurer and took risks. He thought he would give Peru a shot and wanted to find out about the rubber business in Peru—entrepreneur that he was. It was a glorious time to be in Peru if you were friends with the White Peruvian circle which included Prime Minister Larco Cox. Grandfather Lippincott most certainly was a member of that group. Abuelo Juan Lippincott never became a politician nor did he make a huge fortune in exporting rubber like many of the White Peruvians from England. But, he made enough to feed his family and establish himself in Iquitos, the capital of the rubber boom from where rubber was exported to all parts of the world by the Peruvian Amazon Company. Most people don't know about the importance of the British migration to Peru and Chile in the latter part of the 19th century, and the fact that Lima was then a part of what was called the Viceroy of Peru."

Suddenly Oskar saw that the beautiful sapphire orbs of her eyes were covered by her thick dark lashes as he finished speaking. Oskar began to swoon as he stood in front of the ballerina, and without realizing it he murmured aloud, "She is not a person, but it is a *Morpho aurora lamasi* with her bright blue wings tucked neatly under her body." Involuntarily he began to lift his butterfly net as she opened her eyes and slowly stood to face him.

"Mr. Lippincott, what are you saying? Are you quite well? Why don't you come and have tea with me tomorrow at 4:00? We should be settled into our respective quarters by then."

He self-consciously lowered his butterfly net and replied, "I'd be delighted to have tea with you, Madame Castellanos de Varga and shall look forward to it."

* * *

Oskar arrived carrying a small bouquet of lavender sweet peas and rang the bell which responded immediately with the sound of a carillon of soft chimes. He listened in rapt attention when Maria suddenly appeared at the door dressed in a flowing blue silk tea gown. Oskar remained open-mouthed for almost a minute. "Is it a *Morpho portis* I see or do my eyes deceive me? Only in Argentina have I seen such a splendid Blue Morpho!"

"Do come in, Oskar. I don't know what you are talking about."

Maria led him to a splendid tea table filled with a variety of sandwiches, tarts, and small cakes which she offered one after the other to the enchanted Oskar. Their conversation flowed without stopping for the next hour when Oskar stood abruptly to exclaim, "Maria, if I may, I have overstayed my welcome and must leave you immediately. We shall meet again at my humble apartment which does have a small and rather charming garden. At least the butterflies like it very much, and I hope you will also."

The two new residents of the Casa de Harmonia Retirement Community continued to see each other regularly for the next two months. Maria appeared anxious when Oskar asked if she were going to take advantage of the Retirement Home exchange on the island of Martha's Vineyard. "Why would I want to do that when I am at last comfortably settled here in Santa Barbara?" Her eyelashes fluttered as she asked the question directly.

"Because it is a change of scenery for you and therefore life enriching," he replied. "And because I am going, and I would miss having tea with you for three months," he added with a quick smile.

"I am going because I want to catch another excellent species to add to my collection of Blue Morphos, and it thrives in Martha's Vineyard. If you don't come that would make me sad." He smiled at her as bewitchingly as he could muster, twirling his mustache.

* * *

Two months later Oskar removed his sunglasses and looked unblinkingly at the long line of walkers and wheelchairs slowly scuttling onto the ferry bound for Martha's Vineyard. Their happy owners limped along independently behind the procession with only their canes. Oskar lowered his voice because those around him appeared to be listening to their conversation. "Look at them. They appear not have not a care in the world and are loving their newfound independence. Do they not realize that in coming to Martha's Vineyard it is merely an exchange of earthquakes for hurricanes?"

"Oh, Oskar. Must you be such a pessimist? We are going to have a wonderful time and I believe you will find that magnificent Blue Morph you have often talked to me about…the blue swallowtail, the one that lives on the island permanently."

The two-month exchange furlough on the island had begun fortuitously. Some 30 residents of Casa de Harmonia were moving en masse almost without incident to the Vineyard, and an equal number of Havenside Home residents had vacated their homes and moved to Santa Barbara. When they arrived in Vineyard Haven Oskar followed Maria to make sure she got into her assigned cottage. As soon as she arrived, she immediately opened the windows and exclaimed joyously, "Listen, Oskar. The sound of the waves is like a Beethoven symphony. Aren't you happy to be here. It is heaven!"

A big grin appeared on Oskar's face as he turned towards her, "Just being here with you is heaven, Maria. And, of course, finding the perfect blue Morpho, that *Battus philenor* will add to that perfection."

She smiled at him briefly, then changed the subject nervously and abruptly. "Oskar, I must share with you some news I received just before leaving Santa Barbara. It is not pleasant and I hesitated to even tell you."

"What is it, my dear?"

She hesitated, closed her eyes, and finally blurted out, "I have stage four lung cancer! Can you imagine that?" Tears began to fall down her cheeks as Oskar held her in his arms and wiped her tears. They both were suddenly silent, Oskar searching his brain for something consoling to say to her. Finally, he found the words, "We will get a second opinion. Maybe that isn't true, my dearest and loveliest Blue Morpho."

She always laughed when he called her that. "You have taught me so much about the Blue Morphos and one jolting fact sticks in my mind…that they all have very short lives. Unwittingly, I fear I must share that characteristic with them.

Although in terms of years, mine has not been a short life, but I feel it has been short in what I have accomplished. I still have things to see, places to visit and people to love."

Maria did get a second opinion but it matched perfectly the first. Oskar comforted her with his existential philosophy and unabated love. "Maria, we must do something fun every day. I have bought tickets to leave the island and fly to Paris for a week of pleasure. The museums, parks, restaurants, and shops will delight you. You will see."

Indeed, if ever there were a magician who could change moods it was Oskar. He arranged everything, including the afternoon siestas when Maria picked up steam and was again ready for a new outing designed by Oskar. Her favorite was the short trip out to Giverny to see Monet's beautiful garden of iris and his spectacular water lilies. When they celebrated their meeting anniversary it was at Le Grand Vefour, and Maria wore Oskar's favorite long blue gown.

* * *

It seemed only yesterday that Maria had announced she had cancer but it was actually three years almost to the day that she died a peaceful death in her sleep. Those last three gratuitous years were full of happiness for them both. Oskar continued to capture blue butterflies in Latin America but always remembered his own perfect Blue Morpho, Maria Castellanos de Vargas, until his own death almost a year after she died.

4
The Golden Coffee Cups

There was no name on the return address of the package left at my door, and I was hesitant to open it. But curiosity got the better of me, and as I carefully unwrapped the tissue paper to my surprise there were two beautiful golden cups and saucers that I recognized immediately.

They were the same golden cups Peter and I drank *caffe lattes* from at the Antico Caffé Greco on the Via dei Condotti in Rome. The note included in the box was carefully handwritten. I tore it open to read: "Dear Mrs. Matteson, I read in the newspaper about your golden wedding anniversary this week and remembered the time I saw you and your future husband over fifty years ago at the coffee shop on the Via Condotti. You didn't notice me because the two of you were so engaged in each other, and I was merely an observer at a table near yours. I watched you not with envy because I too had fallen in love with a wonderful man who became my husband for almost 30 years. No, it wasn't envy but I watched with a certain joy in seeing such a beautiful couple in love. Your delight and appreciation of each other were so obvious, and I wondered at the time if you were engaged or if it was just the beginning of a romance. I knew, however, that it would be a lasting relationship, and when I read about your golden wedding anniversary this week and saw your picture in the newspaper, I had to send you the enclosed golden cups as a reminder of your love for each other way back then. It seemed to spread throughout the restaurant because I saw others staring at you too. Enjoy these cups which are the same as those from which we all drank our coffee at the Caffé Greco so long ago. Celebrate with them and perhaps you will remember where you first saw and drank from similar ones in Rome." It was signed "Claudia."

The cups were indeed beautiful and did remind me of those days when Peter was first courting me. But how could I thank this person? I do remember a lovely young woman sitting in a corner and staring at us with her large brown eyes and the beginning of a sweet smile curling on her lips.

It turned out that Claudia was not her real name, and I did wonder why she hid herself from me. It took some sleuthing, but I discovered her real name was Judith Singer also known as Mrs. Italo Calvino, the widow of the famous Italian writer. Who would have thought!!! I loved that man's writing and so wanted to know him because his philosophy resembled mine in so many ways. He was considered a utopian writer for the 1950s, whose writing some considered a sophisticated parody of the poetics of Richardson and parodied by Fielding. Some called his writing magical realism; others called him a post modernist, but I didn't know those terms. I found him to be a gifted and very funny writer, one who was full of good advice and whose love of independence I shared.

I began my sleuthing the day after I received the package with the golden cups. I took the package to the Caffé Greco to show the owner. When I explained that I had received the cups but didn't know who had sent them, and wanted to thank that person, his eyes lit up and he told me he had sold them to a very dear lady who was a frequent customer at the Café. He knew her personally and when he saw the return address on the package he said, "That's my friend Signora Judith's address and she now lives very near here at that address." That was all I needed so I wrote to her at the return address on the package to thank her. To my surprise she answered my letter and asked me to come for coffee at her apartment.

When I arrived at her penthouse apartment on the Via Sistina carrying a bunch of anemones, she greeted me with such genuine affection I felt we had known each other for years.

Her cane and mine clinked against the tile floor as she led me into her living room.

"Claudia, you may put the cups there and we will serve

ourselves," she said in Italian to the girl who had brought the tea service and biscotti into the large living room as we entered. After she left the room Signora Calvino turned to me smiling and asked, "I suppose you want to know why I didn't use my real name on the package I sent you? But you were clever enough to find me anyway."

"I think I know why," I began before she interrupted me.

"My husband and I shared a love of independence as you can imagine. I didn't want you to know me as Mrs. Italo Calvino but as Judith Singer, an unknown person to you from the past who recognized and admired you and your companion for the love you felt for each other." She then gave a little laugh and looked straight at me with her soft brown eyes before continuing, "You see, I am a romantic."

I sipped my coffee from one of the now familiar golden cups before answering her, "Yes, I knew that when I saw those cups you so thoughtfully sent me. You see, those cups sent memories flooding back, of the café Peter and I frequented so often, of the same cups we drank from so often there, and even a vague vision of a beautiful young girl with deep brown eyes sitting at a nearby table staring at us. Don't apologize for being a romantic because I think your being a romantic must be one of the reasons you and your husband felt comfortable together." She nodded and said quietly, "*Appunto*."

"But you weren't married then, were you, in 1960 when I was living in Rome?"

"No. I was just a girl from Argentina, and he was already *molto famoso*."

"You were beautiful; I know that because I have seen a picture of you in those days, and I know he must have appreciated you on many levels."

She blushed. "You are very kind. I suspect you understand the expression '*un colpo di fulmine?*' That is what it was like for us. I think you say: 'love at first sight.' Because we were both so very busy, we didn't marry right after our meeting, but it was two years later in 1964 that we married."

I couldn't help interjecting, "Just a year before Peter and I were married! Ours too was a colpo di fulmine. I knew right away that I wanted to marry him, but it took two years before that happened." I too was now blushing at having tried to make such an irrelevant connection with her.

Sipping our coffee, we spoke of many things: of the acute sadness in living without our husbands, of the lives we lived both during our courtships and even during our marriages. And, of course, about our children. We both smiled as we remembered the laughter these two men had brought into our lives. It was as if I had known Judith Singer as a close friend forever, and what a pleasure it was to talk to her! But I felt I had overstayed my visit. As I rose to leave, she touched my elbow, "We must meet again." Her voice quivered as she ended our visit, "I am so glad you responded to the golden cups."

The next week I read in the *International New York Herald Tribune* that Judith Singer, wife of the late Italo Calvino, had died in Rome after a short illness.

5
Casa de Harmonia Resident Experts

"Mrs. Castle, I understand you are a restaurant critic. I too am a food critic and have had vast experience. Perhaps we should talk."

The tall white-haired man stood looking down at the petite Mrs. Rachel Castle, retired food editor at *Gourmet* Magazine who smiled showing her glistening white teeth, "Of course."

"You say you have had vast experience. I am sure I can learn from you. Where have you had this vast experience?"

"All over the world. I know about Chinese food, Indian food, French food (which is overrated I believe), Italian and Japanese food. I can cook and have already cooked most of the best dishes from those cultures. You name it and I'll cook it for you. For example, no one can make a better braciola than I, Pierre LeMoyne."

"I see, Mr. LeMoyne. I have written about the wonderful braciola at what I think is the best Italian restaurant in New York, Falidia."

"Yes. Falidia is very good but *MY* braciole are better, they say. And I'd love to prepare the dish for you and some of your friends." He delivered this response with his best charming smile.

Two weeks later, at 7pm, Mr. LeMoyne welcomed six guests including Mrs. Castle at his Casa de Harmonia apartment. They were all dressed appropriately in their most festive attire. Mrs. Castle's low cut velvet décolletage captured the attention of everyone. Three of the guests seated themselves on the curved Art Deco sofa before Pierre served champagne and gave a brief introduction about the menu. The scent of toasted pistachio nuts and roasted tomato sauce filled the room while Pierre smiled with pleasure as his guests strolled about the apartment, admiring the exquisite furniture and art. The glass top rectangular table in the dining room was set for six with period silver and Art Deco wine glasses at each place and the table was surrounded by six comfortable white high back chairs in the Art Deco style.

Not twenty minutes later an anguishing scream was heard from the kitchen. One of the guests, Dr. Rumplemeyer rushed to the kitchen where he found LeMoyne with a bleeding hand moaning in pain. After applying a makeshift tourniquet, he dialed 911 for an ambulance to deliver Mr. LeMoyne to the hospital. The guests though stunned by the dramatic circumstances in the kitchen helped themselves to more champagne and rose to the occasion directed by Mrs. Castle. "Mr. LeMoyne has almost completed magnificent Braciole which I will finish roasting since he had to leave so unceremoniously after cutting himself to the point of almost losing a finger! He is being cared for at the hospital, and I am pleased to report that he will not lose his index finger. After having the necessary surgery, he will spend the night in the hospital and has requested that we continue to dine here at his apartment. I will need one of you to help get the main course on the table in twenty minutes when I am sure the Braciole will be ready. Meanwhile will one of you open the San Giovese, and we will begin with Mr. LeMoyne's Stracciatella which smells delicious. It is a soup designed to comfort, and we all need that right now."

The guests gasped with delight when they saw the next course, layers of perfectly flattened steak, covered with a filling of pine nuts, softly browned panko and a mixture of Parmigiano-Reggiano and Pecorino Romano cheeses. Each steak had been rolled up, cut in half and tied securely so that the filling was contained under the rich tomato sauce and draped with thinly sliced prosciutto. Next came the dessert, a *piece de resistance* of chocolate and almonds which had been prepared by their absent host, finished by Mrs. Castle and enjoyed until around 10:00, an unusually late hour for the residents at Casa de Harmonia.

The next day as Pierre LeMoyne returned to his apartment at the retirement home his phone was ringing. He rushed to answer

"Yes. This is Pierre LeMoyne, former food critic."

He heard a familiar voice respond. "Why do you say *former* food critic? I thought you felt assured of that position and you were so confident. Nonsense! That happens to the best of us. It was a perfect *Braciola* and you should be proud."

"My dear, you are so kind—particularly for a food critic. After that fiasco in the kitchen I will never call myself an expert at anything. Even a sous chef!"

"Now Now, Mr. LeMoyne. We all appreciate you, and look forward to your next creative dinner, without the drama in the kitchen. Food critic you *might* be, but chef you definitely are."

6

The Story of Micky McKee
from Cook to Chef via the US Army

When my fiancé Pierre who was French first met Micky, it was in his kitchen. Micky was a chef and we were thinking of having him do the food for our wedding reception. It was to be a *fête champêtre* in the pergola built by my grandparents at the base of a waterfall on the banks of the Hudson River. Micky sat us at the kitchen table and slid a crock of rillettes down the table in front of Pierre. He poured us each a glass of wine and said, "Dig in and tell me what you think." I had never tasted rillettes before and never even heard of them, but Pierre smiled with pleasure at the first bite. He looked at me and said, "This is absolutely perfect. I could imagine nothing more suitable." Mickey beamed with pride and announced there would be very little else. "Good champagne, a wedding cake, and excellent French bread for the rillettes. Perhaps a variety of French cheeses and toasts for those who don't eat meat," he added.

And then, Pierre asked, "Where did you learn to make those fabulous rillettes? And tell me about your career."

Micky, already liking this fellow, was not shy and began his story by saying "Well, I loved to eat, and my mother was not only a fabulous person, but she was also a magician in the kitchen. My two sisters and I spent our summers on the island of Martha's Vineyard in a small three-bedroom house we called 'the camp', surrounded by water from the Vineyard Sound that came nearly up to the front porch, and looking out the kitchen window in the back of the house one could see a lake filled with clams and mussels which we gathered regularly. The camp had been built by our father who was a Californian and who left us after a few years to return to California. But that is a different story." He paused, looking as if he were in a different world and then began again, "When I was eight years old, I began helping Mama prepare the beach plum jelly she always made tons of to sell at the Vineyard Haven Fair."

Micky produced another delicious dish as if it were magic. From the oven he brought us a spectacular quiche Lorraine before he continued to reminisce. "Since there was no running water in the camp and no electricity we had to go into Vineyard Haven to fill water jugs for fresh drinking water and cooking. We flushed the toilet with buckets of sea water. It was all a great adventure for us children, and I remember how happy we all were—particularly our mother. After our father left, our mother filled his shoes, and we were never bored with her stories, her new things to do on rainy days and her food that always delighted us. We really didn't miss him much because there were countless cousins, and my mother's sisters and brother, and of course our wonderful Granny—all of whom we loved and who filled our days with adventurous new things and lots of laughter.

My mother had a bad heart, and one autumn day after the beach plum jelly was made when we had all gone back to our boarding schools, she died."

Micky suddenly stopped talking, took a sip of wine, and sat down at the table with us.

"Don't continue, Micky, if this is too sad for you," Pierre said.

"No. I want to tell you why I am a chef. It's because when I cook, I know my mother would be proud of me, and I feel close to her. That makes me happy," he smiled.

"But there are more people who helped me find myself and decide on the career I wound up having," he chuckled. "After I graduated from college, I had no idea what I would do. I had enjoyed learning French and loved my French teacher and his family. I made him laugh and I loved that because I had always loved entertaining people. I loved hearing him talk about the food he ate when he lived in France.

I wanted to know everything about every course. What was served first? How were the meals designed? What was the décor in the restaurants? And finally, how could I get a job that would take me to France where I could taste those culinary delights? My mouth watered when he described the roast leg of veal, the squab roasted in butter fresh from the oven, and served with crispy rissolé potatoes. And my stomach rumbled in response to his description of the apple tart *flambé au calvados*."

The phone rang several times before Micky finally ran to answer it, and we could hear him speaking excitedly. "Who did you say would be there? Really? THE Elizabeth Taylor? Of course I'll be there." He returned to the kitchen table almost dancing.

"You never know who you'll meet when you're a chef. Where was I? Oh yes planning my career with my French teacher in college so that I could eat those wonderful dishes—that was my only goal at the time, I think.

"I believe Mr. Macon, the French teacher, was having as much fun as I was—planning my life. We decided that since I loved to entertain and to cook, the hotel business might be a possibility. After college I was hired at the Hotel Raleigh in D.C. as an on-the-job trainee for $20 a week and was to work in all parts of the hotel. I worked, beginning in the kitchen, in all sections: first roasting, which included all kinds of meat and poultry and fish. And also, a stint for two weeks in the patisserie section under a very fastidious chef who only allowed me to make melba toast, and I wasn't allowed to touch anything else.

"I never got to the sauce section because the Korean war had begun, and I was drafted and sent to Camp Cook in California. When the company warrant officer in charge of the mess hall learned I had worked in the kitchen of a hotel, he asked me if I would be the company cook. The food was so awful I knew I could make it better so I said yes, but only if he would let me cook with wine. I bought a copy of Betty Crocker's cookbook, studied it and the next day at 6:00am I was in the kitchen when the warrant officer arrived with three gallons of wine. After the breakfast for 170 men of the Heavy Mortar Company, the mess sergeant told me to cook chickens for lunch. There were fifty chickens in the freezer which I cut into quarters and threw into large roasting pans with some vegetables. Then I remembered some of Betty Crocker's ideas and a few of my own, and of course the wine. It all came together and the aroma was incredible. The boys loved it and I was amazed at my success. From California my platoon was sent to Japan where I was flabbergasted by the beauty of the food there. Our company spent nine months in Sendai at Camp Schimmel Pfennig. There we had a battalion mess which meant we had to feed five hundred men.

The last part of my time in the service was spent in Korea where I could use my imagination as a cook to make awful food taste good. It was then that I knew what I wanted to do when I became a civilian again. But I also knew that I had to be a better cook in order to be a good chef and that meant going to France."

* * *

We did insist that Micky continue the story but only after he took a break. He agreed to have dinner with us at the restaurant of his choice. We learned that night that Micky did in fact go to France on the GI bill where he started at the prestigious Cordon Bleu cooking school and which he found to be unsatisfactory for what he wanted. A French friend got him a job in a restaurant in Lyon called Chez Nandron. From there he told us he made the decision which would be the best career move of his life. Micky had a huge grin on his face when he uttered the next words. "I somehow intrigued and impressed the chef and owner of the best three-star restaurant in France which at the time was Restaurant de la Pyramide in Lyon. I offered to wash dishes or anything else the chef needed if I could work in the great Monsieur Point's kitchen. From that first meeting and the next two I showed Monsieur Point how dedicated I was, how hard I could work, and gradually he worked way up to being the head sauce chef at the restaurant."

After two years he knew it was time to return to the U.S. to make his way in the competitive world of restaurants in New York City. First, he worked as chef at the Jupiter Island Golf Club Restaurant in Hobe Sound, Florida, then at a few more restaurants in the States including a year at Brussels in New York and the Waldorf-Astoria. He eventually tired of the drudgery of cooking for such large numbers and returned to what he loved: teaching. At the extension office of the University of California at Los Angeles he was offered a job which grew to teaching six sessions a week of 30 students in each session.

His catering business soon became so lucrative he could afford to quit working in restaurants and devote his time exclusively to catering and to the writing of a cookbook *Love, Tine and Butter*. He was also teaching cooking classes to a few suburban housewives. All of these helped him to at least feed his family, but after a time there was no real satisfaction in any of it and he wondered why. A psychiatrist he had been seeing for a few years concluded, "I've figured out what your problem is, Micky. People are eating your art." Micky thought this was hilarious and told everyone around him of that psychiatrist's conclusion. He'd laugh, have another drink, and shake his head. Unfortunately, neither he nor the psychiatrist could do anything about the sadness he felt, nor his lack of self-esteem. He died a sad old man who never acknowledged that he had already reached his goals, and even though he had made other people happy, that was not enough. Fulfillment was never his to be had.

7

The Search for Approval

Our California grandparents came to visit us in Texas once a year when we were children. Our grandfather was a lovely man who listened carefully and seemed interested in whatever we said. Our grandmother, on the other hand, always had something critical to say about us and to us. "You children make so much work for your mother. And you're so noisy." One day she actually said, "I really don't like you children. Maybe when you grow up, I will feel differently." That really hurt my feelings because I thought everyone liked us. Certainly, our other grandmother from New York liked us. She even said she loved us. I wondered how grandmothers could be so different.

I even tried a few times to make my three brothers be quieter when she was in the room. They were being good and quiet for almost ten minutes, about as long as they could stand it. Then one after the other said, "Now can we go outside and yell and laugh and have some fun?"

We were rather glad when the California grandparents left to go back home. But we hated to see our grandfather leave. He always drew the nicest pictures for us because he was an artist. I wished my grandmother had been more of an artist. Maybe that would have made her nicer. Or, I thought, maybe when we grew up, she would like us as she had once said to me. I supposed I would just have to wait and see.

* * *

When I was a student at Vassar I wrote her only occasionally because I never seemed to have the time, but I did send her my first piece of creative writing. It was a short story which my freshman

English teacher had said she liked very much. My grandmother never responded to that letter with the short story but much later my aunt told me she had read the story to her literary circle and that she was proud of her granddaughter. That surprised and pleased me beyond words. I wondered though why she herself had never told me.

After I graduated and began to take jobs that took me to foreign countries, I wrote to her from Florence that I was studying Italian and having such a good time. She responded immediately that she had written to her friend Bernard Berenson who was a famous art historian and whom she thought I should meet. He was living near Florence in Settignano at the Villa I Tatti, and she wrote me that it would be an honor for me to go there if he invited me. I did receive an invitation to visit I Tatti, to see the beautiful gardens surrounding his villa, and to meet the famous art historian. Naturally I accepted when the invitation arrived from his office. It stated that I was to be at the Villa punctually at 3:00 and that because he had been unwell, my visit would be limited to fifteen minutes. When I arrived at the Villa I was told to sit in the garden and that he would find me. It was thrilling to see that old man tottering down the path towards me. His first words were welcoming and then, "How nice to receive the granddaughter of my friend Susan Hyde. Are you as sharp as your grandmother? I admired her enormously when she was a student of mine during our younger days. Now tell me what you have seen in Florence."

I told him I had been to almost all of the one hundred churches in Florence and that it was my goal to see all of them. He smiled and said, "That is an interesting idea. Not all the paintings and frescoes are good but you will learn by seeing the inferior ones as well as the best of them. You know, to really appreciate a work of art one must see it in the flesh…not in a photograph."

Before his nurse approached to take him away, he held my arm and said, "The trouble with us is NOT that we aim too high and fail, but that we aim too low and succeed. Don't settle for what is possible. Just aim for what is truly great." I took these words of wisdom to my next job in Venice.

A letter from my grandmother was waiting for me when I arrived at the home of my future employer and family. In the letter she had included a picture of herself with my mother in Piazza San Marco where I was currently living. The photograph showed them each holding some of those pigeons that swoop in whenever they think there is food around. I in return sent her a picture of me, walking in Venice with my current boyfriend. She didn't respond for a long time and I thought she was disapproving of me or of him. I had to be more careful of what I shared with her if I wanted her to approve of me, and for some reason that was still one of my goals when I was in my mid-twenties.

It was after I had returned to live and work in Rome that I received a letter from her that didn't sound like her at all. It was flattering, gentle and it sounded more as if my grandfather had written it. I wondered if he had. In that letter she had asked if I had met Peggy Guggenheim and seen her collection. I wrote back that I had indeed met her and even gone to a couple of parties at her house on the Grand Canal where there were many artists and writers. I loved that group of people and was pleased that my boyfriend, whom Mrs. Guggenheim loved, had made her invite me by saying he wouldn't come to her parties if he couldn't bring me. My grandfather later wrote me a very personal letter explaining that he had told my grandmother that she should be gentler with her granddaughter who loved and admired her. Apparently, she listened to him because her letters at a certain point took on an entirely different tone and were even encouraging. There was almost an apology from her when she wrote for the first time ever that she was proud of me and loved that I was leading such an independent life full of adventures. She said that she regretted she had never before told me as much.

When I returned to America and went to live in California, she was the first person I wanted to introduce to my fiancé. My aunt introduced him to her as Dr. Dorra since he was a professor. My grandmother immediately turned away from him and stared rigidly out the window, and never uttered another word. There was an embarrassing silence in the room until my aunt explained to her that he was not a medical doctor but a professor of art history. She suddenly turned back into a charming conversationalist when she learned he had not been summoned to examine her. She even smiled gently at me, nodding in approval of my choice in Henri.

In some ways she never changed, but for me her approval was what I was thrilled to see.

8

Otero goes Round the World but Always Back to Venezuela

My name is Estudio para Coloritmo 3, and I was painted as a study for a large collection of seventy-five Coloritmos: abstract works made with Industrial Dupont paints called Duco. My strong primary colors against a white background are on a rectangular wooden board that is five feet seven inches tall and 17 inches wide. I was painted by the Venezuelan artist Alejandro Otero.

I was shown in an exhibition of new works by my still fairly unknown creator in a gallery in Washington D.C. in 1956. At that time a young curator at the Corcoran Gallery, Dr. Henri Dorra saw great promise in my work and understood that I was emphasizing rhythm and color over form and content. He bought me at first sight. He was finishing a huge work with John Rewald: the catalogue raisonné of George Seurat with John Rewald. He was also giving lectures on the Golden Section and Charles Henry. At that time in the larger world, Elvis Presley was making his name known with "the Blue Suede Shoes" and "Hound Dog", two records that stayed at the top of the charts for many weeks and made rock and roll and Elvis Presley household words. Of course, none of the art historians knew or cared at all about that phenomenon.

1956 was an election year in which Eisenhower easily won a second term over his Democratic opponent, Adlai Stevenson. I heard lots of conversations at the gatherings Dorra hosted at his art-filled apartments, first in Washington and later in Los Angeles. I saw that many of his friends wore the recognizable Stevenson icon, the silver shoe with the hole in the bottom. I was particularly interested in what they had to say about the seizure of the Suez Canal by Egypt and the forceful responses of France and England. I understood that the U.S. helped negotiate a cease-fire. Cuba too was in the news as Fidel Castro began the revolution there. As a result, a new wave of wealthy Cubans came to Florida with their art collections, and American dealers took even more interest in Latin American art and artists like Otero. I didn't hear Elvis' name mentioned once, but Grace Kelly's wedding to Prince Rainier of Monaco was talked about ad infinitum.

As was true with the works of Vasarely and Léger, spatial ambiguity was particularly important to my creator Otero and the three of them came to be known as Op Artists. Otero made a pilgrimage to the Netherlands to find Piet Mondrian whose work he admired and which influenced him more than any other artist. I liked what most of the critics said about me. One critic at the time wrote that my own work, "with its optical intensity, chromatic vibration, and rhythmic movement against a white background made the picture plane expand outwardly."

When I was in D.C. in the early fifties, my creator met a very attractive Venezuelan artist whose name was Mercedes Pardo. They eloped to Paris where they were married. I know they were happily married and both were at the height of their creative abilities, receiving deserved recognition both in their homeland and internationally. In 1956, two years after I was painted, Otero was awarded the National Prize for Painting in the Venezuelan Official Salon. I was so proud when he represented Venezuela in the Sao Paolo Art Biennial with some of the Coloritmo works.

Henri Dorra owned me and always took great care in transporting me when he moved from Washington, D.C. to Philadelphia and then to California. Even though Sotheby's had been calling my new owner at least twice a year to try to persuade him to sell me, I was surprised when the Sotheby's representative called the Dorra household to say they were having an auction and would like to have me in it. He mentioned that another of Otero's Coloritmos had been sold in the last Latin American auction for $250,000. I knew I was a better painting than that one and that was proven to be true at the auction where I fetched an even higher price. More importantly to me were the words I heard at the auction coming from the mouth of a beautiful Venezuelan woman who said, "I'd love to have that vertical Otero Coloritmo study in my living room in Caracas. It would really fit with the Vasarelys and the Mondrian we just acquired." I thought to myself, That's pretty elegant company I would be keeping and I loved the idea of returning home. It was clear to me that the rich Venezuelans wanted their art back in their country and were prepared to pay whatever was necessary.

I know the Sotheby's representative was enormously surprised when he came to collect me. As he carried me out of the house, I heard him murmur "what I don't understand is what is a painting like this doing in Carpinteria!" Little did he know that my owner had a very good eye for contemporary art and just happened to be living in Carpinteria, California.

But that's not the end of my story. The husband of the elegant lady who bought me said to her when he saw me hanging in their fashionable Caracas apartment, "I'm not sure why we paid so much for that hard edged op art. Let's go to our Modern Art Museum to see if he is represented there and then I will feel better. Or at least we should check to see if he is represented in any of the other art museums in the city."

The wife looked at him in desperation, "But I love this painting and I don't care if Otero is represented in any museum. When I look at our Coloritmo study it makes me want to dance. Those colors are so strong and so vibrant, and they are quintessentially Venezuelan, don't you think?"

The husband nodded in agreement and smiled at his beautiful passionate wife, "Of course."

That made me so happy that she understood me so completely. I was finally where I belonged…hanging in the sophisticated apartment of someone who loved me for what I am and being back for good in the place of my birth again for the rest of my life.

Germination, c. 1890-96, Odilon Redon, (1840–1916), MOMA.

9

Fertility Symbol Et Al

I am part of a collection of valuable black chalk and charcoal drawings now safely ensconced at the Museum of Modern Art in New York City. My journey to that famous museum began in Paris where I was drawn by the French Symbolist artist Odilon Redon between 1890 and 1896. The Gallery dealer Jacques Seligman acquired me in 1951 for his gallery in New York on West 36th Street, where a few years later in 1956 I was bought by a young curator from the Corcoran Gallery in Washington, D.C.. He had an interest in Symbolist art and saw that I belonged in my creator's Noir Group. I was one of the few in that group that was not a monster. I was drawn in various shades of black and became an expression of my creator's inner feelings. He loved black and wrote that "Black is the most essential color…It should be respected. Nothing prostitutes it. It does not please the eye and does not awaken sensuality. It is the agent of the spirit much more than the splendid color of the palette or the prism." A recent critic hit the nail on the heard when she wrote "For Redon, the use of black and white in the fabric of a work had an unexpected way of expanding vision, allowing a 'uniquely visual field' to be reopened…There was an ascetic quality to his blacks that had the capability to shatter and torment, eliciting a revelatory turn inward in the viewer." My creator also wrote "Black and white are, so to say, non-colors that help, by distinguishing the others, to be restful to the eye, to refresh it, just when it could be tired by extreme variety as well as by extreme magnificence."

After framing and hanging me in his D.C. apartment, my young curator always kept me covered with bath towels to keep me from fading. I really didn't like those towels and was very pleased when years later in 1965 in California his wife replaced the towels with matted photographs of beautiful Greek temples.

Those were removed when they had guests so that they could enjoy me. Although I am a small work of art (only twenty by fourteen inches) and only a black chalk and pastel drawing I know the curator and his wife valued me because for years I was hanging in their California living room over the mantle in the most honored space. Everyone who came to the house admired me and talked about me. One friend commented that not all of my creator's Noirs represented darkness and decadence. I was certainly not one of those but one that represented hope and the power of germination.

When I was reluctantly sold years later for the education of the couple's children, I was sad to leave that family but knew it was for a good reason. The young curator was so despondent at having sold me he told his wife that they shouldn't have let me go. Since she hated to see her husband so sad, the day after I left the house the wife called the dealer who was given the job of selling me to say they wanted me back. Alas it was too late because I had already been sold to E. V. Thaw and Company, the well-known art collector who was determined to have me in his important collection. Although he had the same last name as the infamous killer of Stanford White in Madison Square Garden in 1906, as far as they could determine, that dealer Eugene Thaw was not a relation to the crazed killer named Henry Thaw. Nevertheless, for a brief period I was pleased to be in a collection with such artists as Cranach the Elder, Cézanne, Dali, Delacroix, Van Gogh, Picasso, and countless others more famous than me.

I was an important part of the family in California, and I remember that twice a week before they had children the wife used to come and unwrap me and stare at me for a good half hour. It was like a prayer meeting. Sometimes she even talked to me as if I were a person. She knew I was a fertility symbol and expressed her sadness at not having any children. She said the fertility doctor she had been seeing for a year told her they should consider adoption because she certainly would have been pregnant by now. She told me she and her husband had discussed it and they agreed they would take out adoption papers if she wasn't pregnant by the next month.

When the wife came to see me the following month, she was so happy she could hardly hold the pins to uncover the towels over me. As soon as I was fully uncovered, she burst out loud with the news that she was pregnant. I wished I could have taken credit for this event that had brought such happiness into that house but I couldn't. I was just an onlooker, and a wishful symbol holding the positive thought that it would happen. But maybe that was enough to make it happen, after all.

10

I Am a Portrait by Rene Portocarrero

When the Cuban artist Portocarrero first painted me as a clown it was in Havana before the revolution. Even though I was only a 14 ½" by 10 5/8" gouache on paper I was shown there in a very successful gallery when a lovely Egyptian Jewish woman saw me on her first trip to Cuba. She looked into my eyes and could see my soul. Although Portocarrero gave me a fixed smile she could see that there was a sadness underneath that smile. She understood me, bought me right on the spot, and took me to her apartment in Paris where I remained for the next twenty years. Except for a smiling fat Buddha there were no other works of art in the library of her comfortable apartment in the 8th Arrondissement across from the Parc Monceau. I oversaw her small dinner parties, her charming Parisian friends who came for tea and conversation each afternoon at 5:00. There were many important people who had moved to Paris from Alexandria and whom she entertained. Her husband had moved to New York where he was a successful doctor but she preferred to remain in Paris for the time being.

Eventually I saw her son who came regularly to visit her from London and later from Boston. In the 1970s after he was married and had two daughters, he brought his whole family to live in the apartment while he did research on Impressionist painters. I saw those girls grow up, and watched them entertain their French friends, play cards, laugh, eat gummy bears, and tease each other. Occasionally one of them would look at me and inquire about me. "Is that a clown? Is she trying to amuse us with her juggling?" The younger daughter replied, "She is my companion who hides her sadness under that smile, and we talk to each other before I go to sleep at night. We tell each other our sorrows. My father explained to me that clowns are sometimes sad, you know, and many of them have smiles painted on their faces as that clown has. He told me the artist is saying to us that he understands sadness is as much a part of life as happiness is. To experience it is to be human."

During that time in Paris when the girls were at school, I heard the parents say that they should sell the Paris apartment because the girls were growing up and wanted to travel to other countries instead of returning to Paris every summer. I had even heard the girls talking to each other about going to China, to Viet Nam and other countries in the Far East. I couldn't imagine that, and I certainly couldn't imagine their not wanting to come back to Paris to this lovely apartment.

Later, when that family of mine, and they are my family still, decided to sell the apartment and move all the furniture, works of art and almost everything in the Paris apartment to California, I was carefully packed and moved to the States along with everything else. The little girls were all grown up and the younger daughter never forgot that we had been companions in the Paris apartment and she loved me. She requested of her parents that I not stay in California but go to live with her and her husband in Pittsburgh. You can imagine how pleased and relieved I was that she wanted me in that rainy city where the sun couldn't change the colors of my portrait the way it does to other works of art bleached by the strong California sunshine. My gouache colors will last much longer than watercolors would.

The Pittsburgh winters agree with me and I believe my creator Portocarrero would be happy to know that I am in such a pleasant, comfortable place where my owners take care of me and appreciate me whether I am smiling or hiding my sadness when I am not so happy, and I'm still juggling. I also am continuing to watch over the guests who come to our house and who admire me. They are often doctors because the little girl who loved me in Paris is now a grown-up person who has become a doctor, and she has many friends who are doctors, and they all come to her house in Pittsburgh, and I have seen them point to me and heard them admire me.

Coloritmo 3 (study), 1956, Alejandro Otero
(1921–1990).

Bio

Mary Tonetti Dorra (Mrs. Henri Dorra), who has lived in Santa Barbara for over 50 years, grew up in Fort Worth, Texas. She graduated with a BA degree in Philosophy from Vassar College in 1956. Mary lived in Italy for three years where she studied at the University of Florence and then worked as a research-reporter in the Rome bureau of Time-Life. Upon returning to this country, she attended graduate school at UCLA, obtaining a master's degree in Italian. She taught Italian at UCLA, then at the University of California, Santa Barbara in 1965. The Dorras have lived part time in Paris since their marriage in 1965.

Since 1980 Mary has written travel articles for *Gourmet Magazine* and the *New York Times* as well as garden articles for *HG*, *House Beautiful*, *Elle Décor*, the *Los Angeles Times Magazine* and for *Travel and Leisure*. An article "Colonial Kitchen Gardens: A National Legacy" appearing in the April 1993 issue of *Gourmet Magazine* was the genesis for her first book, *Beautiful American Vegetable Gardens*. Her second book, *Beautiful American Rose Gardens* was also published by Clarkson Potter.

Her third book, *Demeter's Choice, A Portrait of My Grandmother* was favorably reviewed by Kirkus: "…Dorra does a terrific job of providing a sense of place as Lawrence explores each new city. We can taste the fresh baguettes in Paris and see the picturesque canals in Venice…Lawrence visits Rodin at his Paris studio and sees her future husband at a ball hosted by Charles Dana Gibson, yet these other artists don't overshadow her achievements…An elegant tale of a female trailblazer whose remarkable story deserves a wide audience."

Two Lives on Four Continents, A Double Memoir was published in 2020 and her fifth book, *I Am a Portrait, Flash Fiction and Other Short Stories* will be available on Amazon in December 2024.